Set Sail for PANCAKES!

WRITTEN & ILLUSTRATED BY

TIM KLEYN

VIKING

Early one morning, Margot came downstairs.
"My tummy is grumbly for pancakes, Grandpa!"

Grandpa nodded.

His tummy was also grumbly for pancakes.

"Uh-oh, Grandpa!" said Margot. "We don't have any

eggs,

or milk,

or flour."

Grandpa unrolled a map. "Hmmmm," he said.
He pointed to the places they would need
to go to gather the ingredients.
Chicken Island.
Cow Island.
And Flour Mill Island.
"Set sail for pancakes!" shouted Margot.

Their boat, *Beluga Blue*, sat in the water. They checked its motor, lights, and fuel. They stored rope, baskets, and extra life jackets. They tied their dinghy, *Baby Blue*, to the stern. The seagulls wished them luck.

Caw!

Caw!

"All aboard!" said Margot.
Grandpa cast off the lines, and with a *TOOT TOOT*,
they were on their way.

Ahoy! Chicken Island!
"Do they have yummy eggs here,
Grandpa?" asked Margot.
"The best of the best," he replied.

Some eggs were in grass. Some in bushes. And some in trees.

Soon their baskets were full. Grandpa tossed some coins in the money jar and they were all set to go.

"Thanks, chickens!"
"Bok bok BOK," replied the chickens.

Ahoy! Cow Island!

"Do these cows make yummy milk?" asked Margot.

"Oh," Grandpa replied, "the best milk in the whole wide sea."

"Hi, cows," Grandpa said . . . but the cows just stared.

"Mooo!" moo'd Margot.

"Mooo!" moo'd the cows.

"You speak cow?" Grandpa asked.

"Doesn't everyone?" she responded.

They milked the cows and were on their way.
Toot toot!
"Thank you, cows!"
"Moo! Moooo!"

Just one ingredient left! Flour from Flour Mill Island.
And just in time. The sky was grumbly like their tummies.

Grumble

Rumble

Grumble

Ahoy! Flour Mill Island!

Grandpa looked at the clouds.

"Looks like I'll need to batten down the hatches."

"Go ahead, Grandpa," Margot said. "I can get the flour."

Grandpa nodded. "I'll row back as soon as I'm done."

Margot walked through the muddy wheat field to the old mill. The building was a little eerie. Margot grabbed a bag of flour and headed back through the field . . .

until her boots got stuck.

Squish!

Shlop!

Squash!

Grandpa came running in a big silly raincoat.
He swooped Margot out of the mud and
slung the bag of flour over his shoulder.

They hustled back to the dinghy as the rain
drip-drop-dripped down, down, down.
"Let's try to get home before the storm," said Grandpa.

Grumble

Rumble

Grandpa saw a flash of lightning in the distance.
"We'll need to find a safe place to wait this out," said Grandpa.

Grumble

Crack

He steered *Beluga Blue* into the first harbor he could find.
They set anchor and hurried into the cabin.

Grandpa sighed. Margot fidgeted.
They waited and waited . . .

until Grandpa had an idea.

"Did you know you can call for help from any banana?" he asked, dialing a number and handing it to Margot. *"Beep boop boo-boop."* Margot giggled. "Hello, yes, my grandpa and I are in a very scary storm. Mm-hmm. OK. Yes. Thank you!

"The storm will be over soon," Margot told him.

Grumble rumble grumble. Grumble rumble grumble.
Drip . . . drip . . . shhhhhhhh. Soon everything was quiet.

Margot opened the hatch and slowly peeked outside.
"Grandpa, look! Come quick!!"

They had not anchored *Beluga Blue* at just any old place. No, they had anchored at the marvelous, excellent, absolutely stupendous Banana Tree Island. "Yummm!" said Margot.

Pretty soon they were peeling bananas,

cracking eggs,

and stirring the batter.

Margot and Grandpa made the
best banana pancakes that anyone
has ever made in the history of pancakes.

They ate and ate and ate until there were
no more hungry tummy grumblies.
"What do you think, Grandpa?" Margot asked.
"French toast tomorrow?"

THE BEST BANANA PANCAKES IN THE HISTORY OF PANCAKES

Prep: 10 minutes
Cook: 10 minutes
Total: 20 minutes
Servings: 6
Yield: 12 pancakes

Ingredients:

1 cup all-purpose flour
1 tablespoon white sugar
2 teaspoons baking powder
¼ teaspoon salt
1 egg, beaten
1 cup milk
2 tablespoons vegetable oil
2 ripe bananas, mashed

Directions:

Step 1
Combine flour, white sugar, baking powder, and salt. In a separate bowl, mix together egg, milk, vegetable oil, and bananas.

Step 2
Stir flour mixture into banana mixture; batter will be slightly lumpy.

Step 3
Heat a lightly oiled griddle or frying pan over medium heat. Pour or scoop the batter onto the griddle, using approximately ¼ cup for each pancake. Cook until pancakes are golden brown on both sides; serve hot.

Dedicated to Stacy and Lucie.
May your tummies never get too grumbly.
—T. K.

VIKING

An imprint of Penguin Random House LLC, New York

First published in the United States of America by Viking,
an imprint of Penguin Random House LLC, 2022

Visit us online at penguinrandomhouse.com.

Library of Congress Cataloging-in-Publication Data is available.

Manufactured in Spain

ISBN 9780593404294

1 3 5 7 9 10 8 6 4 2

EST

Design by Opal Roengchai
Text set in Gill Sans
The illustrations in this book were created digitally.